W9-BJC-074

The
Math Bee

by Delores Lowe Friedman
illustrated by Bill Farnsworth

 HOUGHTON MIFFLIN   BOSTON

Saturdays were always busy at the Gordon house. Mom was up and out to work just as the sun began to fill the sky. When Dad woke Portia at nine, she pulled the covers over her head.

"Just let me sleep a little longer," she begged.

"Chores!" said Dad.

Portia did the dusting. Dad mopped the kitchen floor. Cleaning with Dad was fun because he always made up funny games to pass the time.

"Suppose you had four arms," he said, with a gleam in his eye.

"How many fingers would I have? Twenty," she said before Dad could continue.

"Good answer, but I was thinking you could dust two times faster. You sure would be funny-looking," Dad said.

"Oh, Dad," Portia said with a sigh.

Just then the phone rang. Dad answered it.

When Dad hung up, he said, "Portia, I have to go to the airport. They're having some trouble landing the planes. Why don't you come with me?"

"Is it dangerous, Dad?" asked Portia. "Is a plane going to crash?"

"No, honey. I just have to look at some numbers and figure some things out," Dad answered.

At the airport they drove right to the control tower.

Inside were huge windows where the air traffic controllers could watch the planes they were guiding.

"Look over there," said Dad as he pointed out a window. "A plane will land on that runway in exactly three minutes."

Portia looked back out at the runway. Before she knew it, there was the plane!

Portia said, "Wow, how did you know?"

"I knew how high up the plane was, how fast it was going, and how long it usually takes for a plane to land," answered Dad. "Just a big math problem, really."

On Monday, Miss Frew told Portia's class, "Next month the school is having a math bee for the fourth-grade classes. It will be like a spelling bee, but with math problems."

I love math, Portia thought. I hope I can be in it.

"I think a team from our class can win," Miss Frew said. "If we do, we'll have a pizza party!"

"That sounds great, Miss Frew," said Portia. "I want to be on the team, but I don't think I know how to win."

"That's okay," said Miss Frew. "I'll be your coach. The math team can come to school early every morning. We can study together."

When Portia got home, Mom was in the kitchen. "How are you, sweetie?" she said.

"I'm great," said Portia. "We're having a math bee in school. Miss Frew said she would help us study."

"Your father won the math medal in high school. You should ask him to help you study, too."

For the next several weeks, Portia got up early each morning. She hurried to school to work with three other students and Miss Frew.

Miss Frew taught them many math tricks and shortcuts. She taught them to do math problems in their heads and to work as fast as possible.

The night before the math bee, Dad helped
Portia do the hardest problems she had ever
done. When she solved the last one, she asked,
"Did I get it right?"

"What do you think?" he asked.

"I'm pretty sure I did. The answer just
makes sense."

Then Dad took out a ribbon with a medal on it. "I want you to have this," he said.

"But Dad, this is your medal, and we haven't won the math bee yet."

"I think you have earned it," Dad said, "for all the hard work you did this month. When you work hard and do your best, you're a winner."

The next day, just before the contest, Miss Frew told the team, "You are ready. You studied hard. Just do your best, and you'll be winners!"

Just what Dad said! thought Portia.

EXIT

15

Portia stood close to her teammates on one side of the stage. The other fourth-grade team stood on the other side. The teams took turns solving problem after problem. Finally, the other team gave a wrong answer. If Portia and her teammates solved the problem correctly, they would win. The auditorium was very quiet.

Portia and her teammates worked out the problem. Portia called out the answer.

"That's right!" Mrs. Jackson shouted.

"Pizza party!" shouted Portia's class.

"Count me in!" said Portia.

Dr. Portia B. Gordon-Ketosugbo grew up in Queens, New York. She loved math as a little girl and enjoyed doing problems with her father. He was an award-winning designer of aircraft. Her fourth-grade teacher encouraged math skills with contests and competitions. Portia decided to use her love of math in the field of chemistry. She is now the head of research for a major company.